The Greedy Gremlin

PixieTricks

Read All the Magical Adventures!

Pixie Tricks

The Greedy Gremlin

Written by
Tracey West

Illustrated by
Xavier Bonet

BRANCHES

SCHOLASTIC INC.

For my sister, Katherine Noll, a wonderful writer
who helped and supported me through every step of my
Pixie Tricks journey. — TW

For my children, Daniel and Marti.
You're pure magic. — XB

Text copyright © 2000, 2021 by Tracey West
Illustrations copyright © 2021 by Xavier Bonet

Library of Congress Cataloging-in-Publication Data
Names: West, Tracey, 1965- author. | Bonet, Xavier, illustrator.
Title: The greedy gremlin / written by Tracey West ; illustrated by Xavier Bonet. Description: [New edition] | New York : Branches/Scholastic Inc., 2021. | Series: Pixie tricks ; 2 | Originally published in 2000. | Summary: Sprite and Violet are planning to tackle a particularly large pixie when their attention is diverted to the gremlin Jolt who likes to mess with electrical things, and who has trapped Violet's cousin, Leon, inside a video game; and it is up to the two of them to get Leon, and themselves, out of the game, and Jolt back where he belongs—if they can survive the infamous level eleven.
Identifiers: LCCN 2019044121 | ISBN 9781338627817 (paperback) |
ISBN 9781338627824 (library binding)
Subjects: LCSH: Fairies—Juvenile fiction. | Video games—Juvenile fiction. | Cousins—Juvenile fiction. | Friendship—Juvenile fiction. | CYAC: Fairies—Fiction. | Video games—Fiction. | Cousins—Fiction. | Friendship—Fiction.
Classification: LCC PZ7.W51937 Gqh 2021 | DDC 813.54 [Fic]—dc23
LC record available at https://lccn.loc.gov/2019044121

10 9 8 7 6 5 4 3 2 1   21 22 23 24 25

Printed in China   62
This edition first printing, January 2021
Book design by Sarah Dvojack

Table of Contents

Whenever pixies do escape
Through the old oak tree,
Here is what you have to do
Or trouble there will be.
First find a Pixie Tricker,
The youngest in the land.
Send him to the human world,
The Book of Tricks in hand.
Once he's there, he'll find a girl
Who's only eight years old.
But she's a smart and clever girl
Who's also very bold.
He must ask her for her help,
And if she does agree,
They'll trick the pixies one by one
Till no more do they see.
Only they can do the job.
It's much more than a game.
For if they fail to trick them all,
The world won't be the same!

1

A Breakfast Surprise

"I can't believe yesterday was real," Violet Briggs said out loud.

Violet crunched on her cereal. She stared out the window. Today seemed like any other day. The sun was shining. She was safe at her kitchen table, eating breakfast.

Today wasn't anything at all like yesterday. Yesterday she had met a fairy. A fairy named Sprite. And she had traveled with magic pixie dust. She had saved the world from a tricky pixie named Pix.

"I still can't believe that all of those things happened," Violet said, shaking her head.

Just then, drops of milk splashed in her face.

Violet looked down. A tiny fairy sat on the edge of her cereal bowl. He was about as tall as a pencil. He had green skin and shimmering rainbow wings.

It was Sprite!

"Could I do *this* if I wasn't real?" Sprite asked. He splashed the milk again with his tiny hand.

Violet laughed. "No, I guess not."

Sprite flew in front of her face. "What about this?" His wings tickled her cheeks.

"Okay," Violet said, laughing again. "You're real. But can you tell me again what you're doing here? I'm still kind of confused."

Sprite sat back down on the cereal bowl. "Okay. I'm a fairy. I live in the Otherworld. One day, fourteen fairies escaped from our world into your world."

"Through the oak tree in my backyard," Violet said.

"Right," Sprite said. "Then Queen Mab, the fairy queen, came to me. Because I'm a Royal Pixie Tricker. She said I was the only one for the job, even though I'm new at it. And she said I needed an eight-year-old girl to help me do it. And that's you!"

"And our job is to trick the escaped pixies and send them back to the Otherworld," said Violet.

"Right again. Just like we tricked Pix," Sprite said.

Sprite reached into a small bag around his waist. He took out a tiny book. It was *The Book of Tricks*. The book told how to trick every fairy. If the trick worked, the fairy's magic stopped. And the fairy would be sent back to the Otherworld.

Sprite flipped through the book. "There's something I want to show you," he said.

"One second," Violet said. "I need to make some toast."

Violet got up and put two slices of bread into the toaster. She pressed down on the lever.

Bzzzzz! Sparks sizzled from the toaster! Violet jumped back.

Then . . . *pop*! The two pieces of toast shot up into the air like rockets!

2
A Pixie Plan

Violet ducked as the toast fell to the floor. Sprite flew over to her.

"Why do you have a machine that makes bread fly?" he asked.

"It wasn't supposed to do that," she told him. "It must be broken."

She picked up the bread. Then she sat back down at the table. "I guess I'll just finish my cereal."

Sprite flew to the bowl and picked up a piece of cereal. It was almost as big as his head.

Sprite took a tiny bite of the bright blue cereal. "Not bad," he said. "This almost tastes like fairy food. Is it magic?"

Violet looked at the cereal box. Beastie Bites. Her favorite.

"No," she said. "But the box says it's part of a healthy breakfast!"

Sprite pulled out *The Book of Tricks*. "Before I forget," he said. "Look! Pix is still in the book. We really tricked him."

He opened it to a page that said "Pix." There was a picture of the fairy on the page.

Pix had showed up right after Violet met Sprite. If Pix tapped you on the head, you would forget about work and chores. You would just want to play and play. But Violet and Sprite tricked him. Now Pix was back in the Otherworld.

Violet was glad to see Pix in *The Book of Tricks*. It meant he was back in the fairy world for sure. Before he was tricked, the page was blank.

"I can't believe we tricked Pix," Violet said. "It wasn't easy."

"I think we should try to trick another pixie today," Sprite said.

"Good idea," Violet said. "I'm ready this time."

She pulled her backpack out from under the table. Then she pulled out a whole bunch of things. A flashlight. Mittens. An umbrella. Sunscreen.

"What is all that for?" Sprite asked.

"Well, I know some fairies—like Hinky Pink—can control the weather. So I will be ready if the weather changes," she replied. "I've got other things in there, too."

"That's very clever," Sprite said. "You sound just like a Royal Pixie Tricker."

"Thanks," Violet said. "It's like Aunt Anne always says. It's better to be safe than sorry!"

Aunt Anne

She zipped up her backpack. "Let's do it!" she said. "Let's go trick another pixie!"

3
Leon

"Violet, what are you doing today?"

Violet quickly shoved Sprite into her hoodie pocket as her mom came into the kitchen. She had red hair like Violet. She smiled like Violet, too.

"Uh, I'm going to look for something," Violet said.

Violet's mom leaned over and kissed her on the head. "Your dad and I will be working at the restaurant all day," she said. "Be good for Aunt Anne. And maybe hang out with Leon."

Violet frowned. She and her cousin Leon were the same age. But they did not like to do the same things. And they all lived in the same house. So Mom and Aunt Anne were always trying to get them to do things together.

"Okay, Mom," Violet said.

As soon as Violet's mom left the room, Sprite popped out of Violet's pocket. He smoothed his rainbow wings.

"Ouch!" he said. "That pocket is too small for me!"

"Sorry," Violet said. "Let's go."

Violet ran down to the first floor of the house. Leon and Aunt Anne lived there.

She opened the door to their living room. Sprite hid behind Violet's shoulders.

"Aunt Anne?" she called out.

Leon came out of his bedroom. He was dressed in pajama bottoms and a T-shirt. His dark, curly hair wasn't combed.

"She's in the shower," Leon said.

"Can you tell her I'll be outside?" Violet asked.

Leon shrugged. "Sure," he said. "But let me ask you something first. Were you messing with my video game?"

"What are you talking about, Leon?" Violet asked. "I don't play video games. You know that."

"My controller is all messed up. When I want to go up, I go down. When I want to go right, I go left," Leon said. "If *you* didn't do it, who did?" He sounded angry.

Violet shrugged. "I don't know. Maybe you need a new battery."

"I just put in new batteries," Leon said. "I bet you messed it up when I wasn't looking."

He stepped inside his room and slammed the door.

Violet went outside and into the backyard.

"So that's Leon," Sprite said. "He reminds me of an ogre. They're always in a bad mood."

"That's why I don't want him to help us," Violet said. "He'd spoil everything. Now, let's go find Hinky Pink."

"Right," Sprite said. He took some pixie dust from his magic bag. The dust would take them wherever they wanted to go.

Sprite started to throw the pixie dust.

"Heeeeeeelp!"

Sprite stopped. That voice sounded like Leon.

"He's probably just complaining about his game," Violet said.

"HEEEEEELP!"

"It sounds like he's in trouble," Sprite said.

"You're right!" Violet cried. "Let's go!"

Violet ran back into the house. Sprite flew behind her.

They burst into Leon's room.

Violet gasped.

A scary-looking fairy sat on the edge of Leon's bed. The fairy held the video game controller.

And Leon was nowhere in sight!

Sprite gasped. "Jolt! It's you!"

"What are you doing here?" Violet asked the scary-looking fairy. "And where is Leon?"

The fairy ignored her. He kept hitting buttons on the controller. Then he shouted at the TV screen, "That's it! Almost there! Hee-hee! This is great!"

Jolt was a bit taller than Sprite. He had blue skin, and his blue eyes were streaked with red from staring at the screen. His silvery hair stuck straight up on top of his head.

Sprite flew in front of Jolt's face. He reached into his magic bag and took out a small medal. It said ROYAL PIXIE TRICKER.

Sprite showed the medal to Jolt. "By the order of Queen Mab, I demand that you tell us what you did with Leon!"

Jolt ignored Sprite. "*Action Kingdom* is my favorite game of all time!" he said. "I was playing it all night. Then I took a break to zap your toaster."

"That was you?" Violet asked.

Sprite answered her. "I should have known! Jolt is a gremlin. They love to mess up games and gadgets that use electricity."

Jolt nodded. "I sure do! And when I came back here, a boy was playing the game. I messed with his controller to get him to stop. But he kept playing."

"That boy is my cousin, Leon," Violet said. "What did you do with him? Where is he?"

Jolt paused the game and cackled. "Oh, I did something awesome," he began. "You see, I tried to take the controller back from him. And he started yelling and screaming and making a real fuss. So I took care of him."

Violet was worried. She had seen how some fairies *took care* of things. "What do you mean?"

Jolt laughed and laughed. He laughed so hard, he fell off the bed and rolled around.

"You're going to love this," he said. "It's so funny."

"Try me," Violet said.

Jolt was laughing way too hard to answer. Instead, he pointed.

Violet and Sprite looked at the screen.

The words on the top said LEVEL 1. The picture showed a boy running down a mountain. Big rocks were rolling down the mountain, too.

"What are you pointing at?" Violet asked. "Where's Leon?"

Then Violet noticed something. The boy on the screen had dark hair. He wore pajama bottoms and a T-shirt.

The boy in the game *was* Leon!

5

Action Kingdom

"Get Leon out of there!" Violet yelled at Jolt.

"Why should I?" Jolt said. "He's a selfish little boy. He's more fun in there."

Jolt hit the PLAY button. The picture on the screen started to move. Leon ran down the mountain as fast as he could. One of the big rocks rolled right behind him.

The rock almost hit Leon. Leon screamed and dodged out of the way.

"This level's too easy," Jolt said. "I can't wait to get to level two."

Violet didn't like video games much. But she knew *Action Kingdom*. Leon played it all the time.

The game had twelve levels. The game's character, Action Andy, had to escape a bigger danger in each level.

Leon was already in real trouble. And he was only in level one!

"I don't always get along with Leon, but he's family," Violet told Jolt. "And families stick together. Can you please let him out of there?"

"No way!" Jolt said. "Leon is even more fun to play with than Action Andy."

Violet turned to Sprite. "Do something!"

"Right," Sprite said. He paused. "Uh, what do *you* think we should do?"

"Not again!" Violet said. "Don't you know how to help Leon?"

"I'm not sure," Sprite said. "Remember, I'm—"

"You're new at this. I know," Violet said. "I guess it's up to me."

Violet reached out to take the controller from Jolt.

"Ouch!" A tiny electric shock stung her hand.

"Hee-hee," said Jolt. "You can't take this away from me!!!"

"That was mean!" Violet cried.

"Why don't you try to trick me?" Jolt asked. "That's what you're supposed to do, isn't it? Trick me so I'll be sent back home."

"Sprite!" Violet said. "The book!"

Sprite pulled out *The Book of Tricks*.

"Wait a minute," Violet said. She looked at Jolt. "Why did you remind us about the trick?"

"Because it doesn't matter," Jolt said. "Sprite is the worst Pixie Tricker in the Otherworld. He failed all of his classes."

Violet stared at Sprite. "You failed your classes?"

Sprite blushed. His pale green cheeks turned bright green.

"Not *all* of them," he said.

"Well, it doesn't matter," Violet said. "We tricked Pix, right? We can trick Jolt."

"Right," Sprite said. But he didn't sound so sure.

Sprite flipped the pages of the book. "Here is the blank page where Jolt's picture should be. And here is his rhyme."

Sprite read from the book.

Jolt messes with electric things.

He can zap them with a look!

He'll make your gadgets buzz and zing,

Until he reads words from a book!

"We can only send him back if 'he reads words from a book,'" Violet repeated.

"Hee-hee-hee!" Jolt laughed harder than before. "A book! Imagine that. I've never read a book in my life!"

Violet and Sprite looked at each other.

We'll never get him to read a book! Violet thought. *How will we trick Jolt?*

6

Try Your Hardest

Leon screamed inside the video game. He jumped over a giant rock. He looked like he was really tired. Jolt kept using the controller to make him move.

"We've got to do something," Sprite said.

"I have an idea," said Violet. "But we need to go somewhere."

Jolt laughed again. "Hee-hee-hee! Try your hardest! You'll never trick me!" he said. He didn't take his eyes off the video game.

Sprite flew around Violet's face. "Let's go!" he said. "If you've got a plan to trick Jolt, I want to hear it."

Violet looked at the TV. Leon looked miserable.

"Maybe we should stay and keep Leon safe," Violet said. "What if he gets hurt in the game?"

"Ha!" Jolt said. "I'm great at this game. I never let Action Andy get hurt."

"Never?" Violet asked.

"Well, *almost* never," Jolt admitted. "I always lose the game in level eleven."

The words on the bottom of the screen still said LEVEL 1.

Violet turned to Sprite. "We've got to hurry!" she said.

Violet ran out of the house and into the yard. Sprite flew after her. She stopped at the old oak tree.

"So what's your plan?" Sprite asked.

"I'll tell you," she said. "But first tell me about Jolt. You said that gremlins like to mess up gadgets?"

Sprite sat on Violet's shoulder. "Yes. Like when your alarm clock doesn't go off and makes you late. And your computer crashes. And your car won't start. Gremlins do things like that."

"Do they all like to play video games, too?" Violet asked.

"Just Jolt," Sprite answered. "Once he discovered video games, he loved them. He has more fun playing them than breaking them."

Violet nodded. "That explains Jolt," she said. "But I have a question about *you.* If you failed most of your Pixie Tricking classes, why did the queen send you here?"

Sprite blushed again. "I'm not sure why she thought I was the best pixie for the job," he said. "Unless—"

"Unless what?" Violet asked.

"Unless it has something to do with the poem," Sprite said. "Queen Mab read me a poem before she sent me here."

Violet was excited. "How did it go?"

Sprite's wings twitched. "I can't remember it all."

"Please try!" Violet said. "It could be important."

"It went something like this," Sprite said. "'Find a Pixie Tricker, The youngest in the land. Send him to the human world, *The Book of Tricks* in hand.'"

"Are you the youngest Pixie Tricker in the land?" Violet asked.

Sprite nodded. "Yes. That must be why the queen sent me."

"Okay!" Violet said. "How does the rest of the poem go?"

"I really can't remember," Sprite said. "Besides, we don't have time for this right now. We have to help Leon."

"You're right," Violet said. "We need to go to the library."

"No problem," Sprite said. He took more pixie dust from his bag.

Violet took a deep breath. Traveling with pixie dust always made her sneeze.

Violet held her nose. "I'm ready!" she said.

Sprite sprinkled the glittery pixie dust over their heads.

"To the library!" Sprite cried.

7

To the Library!

Violet's skin tingled. The oak tree vanished.
Rainbow light sparkled all around them.
Then the light faded. Violet blinked.

She wasn't in the yard anymore.

But she wasn't in the library, either.

She was in the mall!

"Not again!" she said. Yesterday, Sprite had landed them in the mall by mistake, too.

"Sorry! I must have been thinking about what happened yesterday," Sprite said. He took out some more pixie dust.

Violet stopped him. "Wait," she said. "Look over there."

They had landed inside the cell phone store. A long line of people waited to get help. They were yelling at the workers and holding out their phones.

"My screen is fuzzy!" one woman said.

"My phone keeps playing the same video over and over," a boy complained.

Violet looked at Sprite. "This is worse than I thought. Jolt must have messed up more than just the gadgets at *my* house. Who knows what else he's done?" she wondered.

"Gremlins cause so much trouble!" Sprite replied. "They mess up everything they can find! When Jolt gets done with *Action Kingdom*, he'll find something new to break."

"Then we've got to hurry!" Violet cried.

"Right!" said Sprite. He threw the pixie dust again.

Violet closed her eyes. She held her nose.

When she opened her eyes, she was in the library. Hanging from a tall bookshelf!

Sprite was hiding
behind a book. He slowly
peeked his head out.

"Sprite," Violet moaned. "Can't you get our landing right just once?"

Sprite popped out and shrugged. "Landing is the hardest part. You can climb down from here."

"Violet Briggs! What are you doing up there?" a voice cried.

Sprite quickly ducked behind the book. Violet looked down. It was Ms. Bowley, the librarian!

8
Books for Jolt

"Uh," Violet said.

"Cleaning the ceiling?" Sprite told Violet in a whisper.

"No!" Violet said.

The librarian looked at her strangely.

"I mean, I was trying to reach a book," Violet said. "And I kind of got stuck. And then I realized I didn't want the book after all."

"Violet, I'm surprised at you. You know better than that," the librarian said.

"Sorry," Violet said. "I, um, just need to get some books. It's really important."

Ms. Bowley sighed. "Well, then you should have asked for help."

She wheeled the library ladder over to Violet. "Here. Climb down," she said.

"Thank you," Violet said. She climbed down from the shelf.

"Now, how can I help you?" Ms. Bowley asked.

I can't tell Ms. Bowley about Jolt, Violet thought. *But maybe she can help . . .*

"I need to find a book for somebody who *really* doesn't like to read," Violet said.

Sprite flew closer and hid behind Violet's head.

"What kind of things does this person like?" Ms. Bowley asked.

"Machines and gadgets," Sprite whispered.

"He likes machines and gadgets," Violet told Ms. Bowley.

"Hmmm," the librarian replied. "Anything else?"

"Video games," Violet said. "He plays *Action Kingdom*. It's full of adventure."

Ms. Bowley walked over to a shelf. "I have a few books your friend might like." She picked out three books and gave them to Violet.

"*Peter Pan* is a classic, and it's action-packed," she said. "*Press Start!* is about a video game character. Oh, and *The Serpent's Secret* has cool monsters in it!"

Violet put the books on the librarian's desk. She took her library card from her pants pocket.

"Thanks, Ms. Bowley," Violet said.

The librarian checked out the books.

"You're welcome," she said. "And please, no more climbing on shelves!"

"Okay!" Violet said. She ran out of the library. Sprite zoomed after her to catch up. Then he settled on her shoulder.

"What do we do with these?" Sprite asked. "Jolt said he would never read a book."

"I don't think Jolt knows how awesome books are," Violet said. "I can read these to him. I bet he'll like them so much that he'll put down his controller."

"It's worth a try," Sprite said. "Let's go home."

Violet and Sprite walked behind a tree. Sprite took out some pixie dust. Before Sprite could throw the dust, Violet gasped.

One of the library books was floating in the air.

Then it flew away!

9
Another Pixie?

"**S**prite!" Violet cried. "What's happening?"

"I'm not sure," Sprite said.

The book flew up high—and landed on the roof of the library!

"No!" yelled Violet.

Then the second book began to float out of Violet's hand.

She tried to grab it, but that book flew away, too.

Violet ran after the book. She noticed that pixie dust was sparkling all around it.

"Pixie dust is making the books fly away!" Violet said. "Sprite, stop doing that!"

"I'm not doing it!" Sprite said. "It must be another pixie. One trying to stop us."

"We have to do something!" Violet said.

Sprite took out his Royal Pixie Tricker medal.

"By the order of Queen Mab," he shouted to the glittering air, "show yourself!"

The second book flew up in the sky. It landed on a high tree branch.

But there was no pixie in sight.

Violet felt the third book twitch in her hands. She held on tightly.

"How do we stop this pixie?" Violet asked.

"We need to find out who it is," Sprite said.

Then Violet and Sprite heard a giggle. It came from the tree.

Violet looked. She saw a flash of purple.

"Who are you?" she asked.

Another giggle.

"Never mind, Violet," Sprite said with a wink. "It's obvious. This pixie is too scared to face me."

"Hey!" came a voice.

A small fairy popped out from behind the tree. She was dressed in a yellow striped shirt and short purple overalls. Wings fluttered on her back.

"Spoiler!" Sprite cried.

"That's me!" Spoiler said. "I'm not afraid of you."

Sprite puffed out his chest. "Well, maybe you should be. I am a Royal Pixie Tricker."

Spoiler rolled her eyes. "Oh please! You couldn't trick yourself!"

Sprite flew up to Violet's ear. He whispered, "Say Spoiler's name backward with me three times. It won't *trick* her. But it will get rid of her for now."

Violet nodded. She and Sprite had done this before.

"So what are you going to do, Sprite?" Spoiler said. "Ooh, I'm *so* scared."

Then Violet
and Sprite
shouted together,
"Reliops, Reliops,
Reliops!"

Spoiler
frowned. "Rats!"
she said.

In a flash, Spoiler vanished.

"Good!" Violet said. "Now we can get back to tricking Jolt."

"Should I fly up and get those books?" Sprite asked.

"Do it fast," Violet said. "We have to go save Leon!"

Sprite quickly rescued the two library books. Then he threw some pixie dust on Violet.

"Achoo!" She forgot to hold her nose.

The library vanished.

55

10
Jolt Escapes

Violet and Sprite were back in Leon's room.

Jolt was still playing *Action Kingdom*. His eyes looked glazed.

"Almost there," Jolt said.

Violet looked at the screen. It said LEVEL 9. The picture looked like a desert. Leon was walking down a sandy trail.

"Leon's still okay," Violet said. "But we have to hurry!"

"This level doesn't look so bad," Sprite said.

Jolt grinned. "Just wait!" He pushed some buttons on the controller, and Leon walked to a hole in the desert sand.

A big snake popped up. It hissed in Leon's face.

"Aaaaaaah!" Leon yelled.

"Whoops!" Jolt said. "I've got to get through this desert without Leon getting bitten by a snake."

Then he paused the game.

"So what are you guys doing?" he asked. "Do you really think you can get me to read a book?"

"No," Violet lied. "I'm just going to sit here and read *my* book."

Jolt hit the PLAY button. "Fine with me. I'll just keep playing the game."

Violet sat on the floor. She opened up *Peter Pan*.

Violet began to read aloud. After a few minutes, Sprite nudged her.

"It's not exciting enough," Sprite said. "Get to a good part."

Violet read as quickly as she could. Jolt ignored her. He kept playing the game.

Violet looked up at the screen. Now Leon was in level ten! It was a jungle filled with pits of quicksand.

My plan has got to work, Violet thought. *Jolt said he always loses the game at level eleven. Then what will happen to Leon?*

Violet read faster. She told the story of Peter Pan. How he brought Wendy, Michael, and John to Neverland. And a band of pirates caught them. The pirates were led by Captain Hook.

Then she skipped to the end of the story. She looked at Jolt. The gremlin had paused the game. He was pretending to play. But he was actually listening to Violet.

"It's working! It's working!" Sprite said in Violet's ear. "Keep reading!"

Violet nodded. She got to the part when Peter Pan and Hook had their final fight.

"'Suddenly, the sword fell from Hook's hand,'" Violet read, "'and he was at Peter's mercy.'"

"You mean Captain Hook was helpless?" Sprite asked.

"Yup," Violet replied. Then she closed the book. "Well, that's it."

Jolt stood up. "What do you mean *that's it*?" he asked. "What happened to Hook?"

Violet shrugged. "I don't know," she said. "That's all there is."

"It can't be!" Jolt said.

Jolt hopped off the bed. He grabbed the book from Violet's hands.

"Let me see that!" he said.

Violet and Sprite smiled at each other.

"Your plan is working," Sprite whispered. "If Jolt reads the book, he'll be tricked. He'll go back to the Otherworld and Leon will come out of the game."

Violet and Sprite waited for Jolt to open the book.

Jolt stopped.

He put down *Peter Pan*.

"Ha!" he said. "You can't trick me *that* easily."

Jolt hopped back onto the bed. He picked up the controller and hit the PLAY button. Then he opened his hand. It was filled with pixie dust.

"See ya!" Jolt said.

Jolt dropped the game controller. Then he sprinkled the glittery pixie dust over his head and disappeared.

"Where did he go?" Violet asked.

Sprite pointed at the screen. "Look," he said.

Jolt was in the video game with Leon!

11
Inside the Game

"There's only one thing to do now," Sprite said, looking at the screen.

"You mean . . . we have to go *into* the game?" Violet asked.

Sprite took out some pixie dust. "Exactly!"

I'm scared, Violet thought. *But it's the only way to save Leon!*

"Let's do it," Violet said. She held her nose
and closed her eyes.

Sprite sprinkled the pixie dust on them.

Violet opened her eyes. She felt weird. Like
she was flat.

Violet looked around. Green jungle plants were everywhere. Big bright flowers grew as tall as she was.

Sprite had done it. They were in the video game!

In the distance, Violet saw Leon running away. Jolt was behind him.

"Over there!" Violet said.

She started to run through the jungle. Sprite flew next to her.

"Violet," Sprite said, "look out for the—"

"Aaaaaaah!" Violet yelled. She had stepped in something soft.

"Quicksand!" Sprite said.

"Help!" Violet said. The quicksand was sticky. It felt alive. It felt like it was grabbing her feet. Now her legs were in the quicksand. She was sinking!

"Oh no! I'll think of something," Sprite said.

Sprite flew around Violet. He grabbed a handful of pixie dust.

Sprite sprinkled the pixie dust on a vine. The vine crawled toward Violet. It wrapped around Violet's waist.

The vine pulled Violet out of the pit.

Then it dropped her onto the jungle floor.

Violet stood up. "Thanks," she said. "Now, let's go!"

Violet ran through the jungle. This time, she kept her eyes on the ground. If she saw quicksand, she ran around it.

Soon they had almost caught up with Leon and Jolt. They were standing in front of a big stone door at the edge of the jungle.

"Leon!" Violet said. "It's me!"

Leon turned around. The look of fear left his face.

"Violet?" he asked. "It's so good to see you!"

But then he looked confused. "How did you get in here?"

Jolt smiled. "No time for reunions. Time to keep moving!"

We're moving on to the next level! Violet thought. *What dangers will we face?*

The big stone door opened, and they all stepped through it.

They walked into a dark space. Torches burned on the red brick walls.

"Where are we?" Violet asked.

"Welcome to level eleven!" Jolt said.

12
Level Eleven

Violet gasped. "Level eleven? That's the one you always lose!"

"That's right," Jolt said. "I always get lost in the maze. But I feel really good about my chances this time!"

74

Jolt dashed into the maze. He ran down a hallway and made a left turn.

"Violet, what's going on?" Leon asked. "And why is that blue guy from my room here?"

Sprite frowned.

I guess we can't keep the secret from Leon anymore, Violet thought.

"The blue guy is a gremlin. He trapped you in this video game," Violet said. "We have to catch him and trick him so we can all get out of here!" She ran down the hallway.

Leon ran after her. "But that's not part of the game!" he said.

"It is now," Violet said. "Hurry up! Follow that gremlin!"

She made a left turn. There was another hallway. Jolt was nowhere in sight.

Leon stepped in front of her.

"Let me lead," he said. "I know this level really well. I can get us through it fast."

"Right. You've probably done this a million times!" Violet agreed.

Violet and Sprite followed Leon. They made turn after turn after turn. But there was no sign of Jolt.

"That blue gremlin guy wouldn't let me play my own game this morning," Leon said. "What's his problem?"

"He just really likes video games," Violet replied.

Suddenly, Leon pulled her down to the floor of the maze.

"Hey!" Violet cried.

Leon pointed up at a giant bird flying overhead. "You have to duck right here, or the hawk swoops down and gets you."

"Thanks," Violet said.

They stood up and kept running. Then they heard a voice: "Drat!"

It was Jolt.

"Double drat!" Jolt cried.

"Over here," Leon said. He made a right turn. Violet and Sprite followed.

Jolt was at a dead end. There was nowhere to turn.

"I hate this maze!" he shouted.

Jolt pounded his fists against the wall. Then he kicked the wall with his boot.

"Stupid, stupid game!" he yelled.

Leon reached into a pocket in his pajama pants. He pulled out a small book: *Action Kingdom Guide.*

"Don't go crazy, dude," Leon said. "Take a look at this. It will tell you how to get out."

Leon tossed the guide to Jolt.

The greedy gremlin flipped through the guide.

"Let's see," he muttered. "Level eleven. Ah, here it is."

Then Jolt started to read from the book.

13
Leon Saves the Day

"**"To** get through the maze, you should—'"
Jolt began to read aloud.

Then he stopped.

A strange wind started to whip around the gremlin.

"Oh no," he said. "It's not fair! This is a *guide*, not a book!"

"Looks like a book to me," said Sprite with a giggle.

The wind formed a large tunnel in the air. The whirling wind pulled Jolt into the tunnel.

"But I don't know how the game ends!" Jolt cried.

The tunnel closed up. Then it disappeared. Jolt was gone!

Violet didn't feel flat anymore. She looked around. She was back in Leon's room. Leon was there, too. So was Sprite.

"Did it work?" Violet asked Sprite. "Did we really trick him?"

Sprite took out *The Book of Tricks.* He turned to the page where Jolt's picture should be. Then he flew up near Violet's face so she could see.

A faint picture was forming. The picture got darker in front of Violet's eyes. Soon Jolt's picture filled the page.

Jolt messes with electric things

"That means we did it!" Violet said. "We tricked Jolt."

"Actually, *Leon* is the one who tricked Jolt," Sprite pointed out.

Violet turned around. Leon stood with his arms folded across his chest.

"What do you mean I tricked Jolt? Was he that blue gremlin guy? And who's the bug?" Leon asked. He nodded toward Sprite.

Sprite flew in front of Leon's face. "I'm not a bug!" he said. "I'm a Royal Pixie Tricker."

Violet took a step back. "Couldn't you just forget this happened?" she asked Leon.

"No way," Leon said. "I almost got flattened by giant boulders. And bitten by snakes. And drowned in quicksand. I can't forget that."

"I guess not," Violet said.

"Besides," Leon said. "If it wasn't for me, we'd still be in that game. That gremlin guy didn't go away until *I* gave him my game guide."

Violet didn't know what to do. *Leon is right*, she thought. *But can I trust him?*

"I can't tell you what's happening," she said. "I just can't."

"Tell me everything," Leon said firmly. "Come on, you can trust me."

Violet looked at Sprite.

"What did you say before? Family sticks together, right?" Sprite asked.

"Right," Violet said. She turned to Leon. "Okay, I'll tell you. But this is top secret."

Violet told Leon everything about the fairies.

"We've tricked Pix and Jolt," she finished. "We've seen Hinky Pink and Spoiler. And there are ten more fairies we have to find."

Leon jumped up. "Okay, then get out of my room!"

Violet frowned. "Why are you being mean? After I just told you—"

"No, I need you out of my room so I can get dressed," Leon said. "We need to get out there and trick some pixies!"

About the Creators

Tracey West has written several book series for children, including the *New York Times*–bestselling Dragon Masters series. She is thrilled that her first series, Pixie Tricks, is being introduced to a new generation of readers.

Xavier Bonet lives in Barcelona, in a little village near the Mediterranean Sea called Sant Boi. He loves illustrating, magic, and all retro stuff. But above all, he loves spending time with his two children—they are his real inspiration.

Pixie Tricks
The Greedy Gremlin

Questions and Activities

Gremlins mess with things that use electricity. What is the *first* electric object that Violet sees acting up?

Sprite explains to Violet that gremlins are responsible for things like broken alarm clocks and cars that won't start. Make a list of other everyday problems gremlins could be responsible for.

Jolt tells Violet that Sprite failed his Pixie Tricking classes. How does this make Sprite feel? How can you tell that he feels this way? Reread page 29.

When Violet and Sprite go to the library, they leave Leon in Jolt's control. How do they know he'll be safe in the game while they are away? Reread pages 33–34.

In the book, readers get to see only what levels one, nine, ten, and eleven of *Action Kingdom* are like. What do you think levels two through eight are like? Draw pictures of each level.